For WWB2, Mooka and Pea
—J.S.

For my best friend, Martin Muscatt
—G.W.

SIMON & SCHUSTER BOOKS FOR YOUNG READERS
1230 Avenue of the Americas, New York, New York 10020
Text copyright © 1994 by Jennifer Selby.
Illustrations copyright © 1994 by Genevieve Webster.
All rights reserved including the right of reproduction in whole or in part in any form.
Originally published in Great Britain by ABC, All Books for
Children, a division of The All Children's Company Ltd.,
under the title *Still of the Night*.
First American Edition, 1994.
SIMON & SCHUSTER BOOKS FOR YOUNG READERS is a trademark of Simon & Schuster.
Designed by Lucille Chomowicz. The text for this book is set in Gill Sans Bold.
Manufactured in Singapore
10 9 8 7 6 5 4 3 2 1

Library of Congress Catalog Card Number: 93-87520

ISBN: 0-671-89571-0

IN THE
STILL
OF THE
NIGHT

BY JENNIFER SELBY
ILLUSTRATED BY GENEVIEVE WEBSTER

SIMON & SCHUSTER BOOKS FOR YOUNG READERS
PUBLISHED BY SIMON & SCHUSTER
NEW YORK LONDON TORONTO SYDNEY TOKYO SINGAPORE

In the still of the night...

COCK-A-DOODLE DOO!

COCK-A-DOODLE DOO!

COCK-A-DOODLE DOO!

COCK-A-DOODLE DOO!

there was a rowdy rooster...

who woke the grunting pigs...

who surprised the bleating sheep...

MOOO MOO

who startled the bellowing cows...

NEIGH

who scared the snickering horses...

who alarmed the

guffawing goats…

who butted the braying donkey...

HONK

HONK

HONK

who bumped the honking geese…

who upset the squawking hens...

SQUEAK SQUEAK

SQUEAK

who scattered the
squeaking field mice...

who tickled the snoring farmer,
who was fast asleep
in the still of the night.

F
SEL   Selby, Jennifer.

           In the still of the
           night.

$14.00

OCT 29		DATE	